CAT IN A BOX

Jo Williamson

SCHOLASTIC

I am a cat, and I have a busy, busy life.
Looking after my family is a full-time job.
They just couldn't do without me!

Each day, I leap in very early ...

…just to **wake them up**.

I never have to bother
with the littlest one.

The twins just need a
softly-softly walkover.
It's the **big** people who
are trouble…

It can take time…

and patience…

but luckily…
I'm the best in town!

We enjoy a spot of **breakfast** together

and I like to sit in my usual place…

just to keep an eye on things.

Then I settle down for my next jobs:

the **washing** and the **drying**.

I never stop!

I guard the house and say hello to visitors. I wonder what's in the post for me today?

It's a box!

All boxes need looking into.

Some are made for **playing peek-a-boo.**

Some are handy for sneaking about.

Some are purrrfect for bouncing into...

...and some are not.

I like the comfy ones best for a quick cat-nap.
I am cat-in-a-box!

Granny often needs some help with her knitting.

But ...

…she doesn't always remember to say 'thank you.'

Afternoons are all about my **hobbies**.

I like to visit the neighbours …

… and have **fun** fishing with my kittycat friends.

Sometimes I feel like a bit of climbing.

I'm a very **playful** cat.

I love to make
new **friends** …

to meet

my
family.

It's always exciting
for everybody.

I don't like to miss out on **anything**...

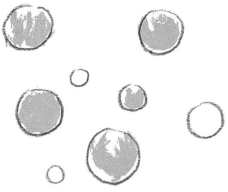

...and often lend
a **helping paw**
at bathtime.

But did I mention...

I'm not too keen on swimming?

Then it's time to fluff and warm myself
up for my last job of the day.
My **favourite** job of the day…

… cosy bed warmer!

My family just **couldn't** do without me.
A cat's life is a busy, busy one …

… and I **love** it.